# The Bridge
## A Collection of Short Stories

By
Paula Kay

# Contents

# Not Today

Laura glanced at her reflection in the rearview mirror as she waited for the light to change.

So tired. She looked so damn tired. And old. And pathetic, she thought as she noticed just how red her eyes were from the latest onslaught of tears that had come during the last hour.

As she had done many late nights before this one, she was making the twenty minute drive to get to the other side of the bridge.

It seemed to help some nights when she was feeling particularly bad. The cold air. The bright lights of the city. She would stare out across the quiet bay, where people were either tucked in their beds sleeping or enjoying a late night drink at one of the city's many bars or night-spots.

She used to enjoy these things too, but not any more.

It had been months since she'd even left her house for anything other than a mandatory shopping trip or a quick run to get some food. Just the bare necessities, and even that seemed to be a daily struggle.

Her thoughts turned to Annie and the quick phone conversation they'd had earlier that day.

*"Mom, are you out of bed? What are you doing?"*

*"Yeah, I'm just doing a little cleaning and getting ready to go out for a bit."*

*"You are? That's great, Mom. Really great."*

She heard something in her daughter's voice.

Annie didn't believe her. She was highly perceptive for her fifteen years, and Laura knew that she was feeling the weight of worry about her mother. She hated that she was doing that to her.

Lovely Annie. She deserved so much more than a mother who could barely get out of bed to shower and brush her teeth.

Annie deserved happier times. Annie deserved everything good and the exact opposite of the sad existence that Laura had lived after her own mother had gone.

God. She could still feel the weight of it. Even after months of therapy. Her therapist really believed that the medication would help her. Even out her mood swings, she had said.

But she hated those pills. They did seem to help at first, but then she couldn't feel anything. Just one big fog.

The drive across the bridge jolted her back to the present.

She could make out the outline of the rolling hills ahead of her. And in the rearview mirror she could see the city lights twinkling back at her.

She pulled into the big parking lot as she had done so many nights before. She knew it would be empty. She especially enjoyed coming to the bridge when no one was around, and tonight was no exception.

Tonight it was the only thing that would take the pain away.

As she turned the car off, her attention went to the necklace she had hung over the mirror before she had left for the bridge. She touched it and remembered the day that Annie had chosen it for her.

It had been a particularly rough morning, but she was determined to keep her lunch date with her daughter. It had been way too long since they'd spent any real time together.

They had gone to one of Annie's favorite Mexican spots in town, and everything seemed to be going fine. Laura had become pretty good at faking it with her daughter. No matter how bad she was feeling on the inside, she tried very hard not to let it affect their relationship. But it had. She knew better.

Annie was in the midst of telling her something about her best friends at dance class when suddenly Laura just burst into tears. —the loud messy kind—and Annie was quickly beside herself with concern.

The intensity of the outburst took Laura by surprise, and there was no time to edit herself as the words came pouring out that day.

"I'm sorry. So sorry, Annie. You deserve so much better. I know I'm not being a good mother to you. I don't deserve you."

After looking stunned and like she didn't quite know what to do, Annie inched her chair close to her mother and grabbed her into a hug.

"Mom, it's okay. It's really going to be okay. You'll see. You're going to get better. You just need to have a little more courage. Do you remember when you and Dad used to talk to me right before my first performances? I would be so scared and talking about everything that I had messed up during rehearsal. I knew I was going to fail, but you would just take my face in your hands and tell me to have the courage to do what I was meant to do. Now you need to do that too, Mom. Please. Do that for me?"

Laura attempted a half smile and thought to herself how amazing it was that she had raised such a young woman. Where did this wisdom come from?

She paid the bill and they left the restaurant.

Not far down the street, as they were walking towards the car, Annie stopped suddenly beside a shop window.

"Wait here, Mom. I'll be right back."

Moments later in the car, she took a necklace out of the bag she'd stuffed in her purse.

The sun emblem shined when she held it for her mom to see before placing it around her neck.

"For when you need a little extra courage, Mom. Think of me and how brave you are."

Tonight in the car, Laura wiped away the tears that were streaming down her face at the memory as her attention turned back to the necklace. She touched the emblem and took a deep breath, wiping the last of her tears away.

She carefully placed the car keys underneath the driver's seat and got out of the car to breathe in the cold fresh night air.

At the last moment, she removed her stocking cap. The nights were quite cold lately, and it could be especially windy on the bridge.

Annie loved this stocking cap. She said it was the perfect shade of girl. A nice light pink that she loved on her mother. Laura opened the unlocked car door and placed the cap on the back seat.

Shutting the door, she was now ready for her night walk to the center of the bridge. She was ready to feel the sense of calm that the bridge brought to her.

As Laura made her way to the entrance of the walking pathway that spanned the bridge, she looked at the city before her that she loved. Or that she used to love, anyways. Before life got so damned hard.

She remembered the early years when she had first met Greg. They had taken this very same midnight walk across the bridge together on many occasions. Talking about their careers, their future, and their love for one another.

Before she had met Greg, she really hadn't known true love. She was so determined during her college years. Determined to succeed, no matter the cost. Determined not to let anything deter her from her future goals. Along with that determination came the resolution that she wasn't meant for love.

Somewhere deep inside her she knew that she wasn't lovable. She knew that love hurt too much, and it was better to count only on herself.

But then she met Greg and everything changed.

She smiled as the seventeen years of their marriage played out in her mind.

The wedding, their successful careers. Having Annie.

Things had been rough, actually, before Annie was born. She'd had moments of depression throughout college, but when things got tough during the first years of their marriage, she didn't quite know how to handle it.

The baby would change everything. That's what she thought when she found out she was pregnant. And they were insanely happy to be having their first child.

More memories flashed before her eyes.

Sweet Annie as a toddler.

Fights with Greg when she couldn't get out of bed to make Annie breakfast.

Day trips to the zoo, parks, museums. Fun family vacations with lots of laughs and pictures to remember them by.

Horrible fights with Greg, and knowing that Annie could hear from her bedroom.

*You need help, Laura. We can't keep living like this. You have a daughter. You have to get out of bed today. Honey, what can I do? We need to call someone and figure this out.*

And through it all…thoughts of her own mother.

Her mother, who had left her when she was only twelve.

Something was wrong when a mother could do that to her child. Something had to be wrong with Laura. Unlovable Laura.

And eventually Greg had had enough.

The separation was quick and firm. He couldn't keep living like this. It wasn't right. He loved her but if she wasn't willing to get help, he was not going to participate any more. That was final.

Her attention snapped back to the cold night air and the dark water in front of her.

She was almost there. Almost to the center of the bridge. It was the spot she loved the most. With the city lights ahead of her and the rolling hills behind, she felt that it was magical. Here she could let go of her problems and just be.

With only steps to go, Laura's heart caught in her throat in recognition of what she was seeing before her. She knew in an instant that she was not alone. And the person she saw was outside of the pathway.

*Oh God. This person is about to jump.*

There was no time to think. Laura prayed the right words would come.

"Please. Don't move. Don't jump."

She tried not to startle the figure by shouting too loudly.

"Don't come any closer. I mean it. Stay away."

It was the voice of a young boy.

"What's your name? I'm not coming closer. Just please talk to me for a minute."

Her heart was beating so hard now. Surely she was about to have a heart attack.

"I don't wanna talk. I'm done talking. I'm done thinking. I'm just done with everything."

His voice caught; he didn't bother to hold back the tears.

"I'm Laura. Can you tell me what your name is? I'm not doing anything. I don't even have my phone. I just want to talk to you, okay?"

"No, just go away! Get out of here!"

"Please, just tell me your name." She knew she had to somehow get him talking.

"God. Please just go away. Leave me alone. I mean it. I'm gonna jump right now if you come any closer to me. Just go away!"

"Okay, okay. Just tell me your name."

"Jake. My name's Jake. Now just leave me the hell alone!"

*God. He couldn't be much older than Annie.* The thought buzzed through her mind.

"Jake, can you just talk to me for a minute? Please. What's going on?"

She willed him to start talking to her.

"I've already decided. I'm doing this. There's nothing you can say that will stop me. Just stay away."

Her heart beat faster. —if that were even possible. What could she say? There had to be something. She wasn't really on a first-name basis with God, but she said a quick prayer in her head.

*Please, God. Show me the words to say to him. I don't know what to do, and I don't want to see this kid die right before my very eyes.*

"Jake. Tell me something. What's going on? Why are you doing this?"

He could have jumped before now, so she guessed that there were doubts in his mind. Or fear. Yes, it would take some courage to do something final. To actually jump. Not everyone had that kind of courage anyways. No matter how dark the days were.

"Just…my life just sucks. That's all. There's nothin' good. Nothin'."

He was sobbing now and she wondered if he was on something.

"What about it sucks? Tell me. I'm just gonna listen. That's all."

She moved forward a little closer as she spoke.

"My dad is being a total dick. Marrying his stupid secretary. They just made this big announcement to me and Chase last night over dinner like it was something we were gonna cheer about."

"Is Chase your brother?" Laura started mentally connecting some dots.

"Yeah, Chase is actually awesome." His voice caught as he talked about his brother, and the sobs came stronger now.

"Tell me about Chase."

She moved a little closer and she could see his face now in the moonlight shielded by his dark hoodie.

"Chase is twelve. He does get on my nerves but I figure I kinda should put up with it cuz…"

"Cuz why?"

Laura knew what he was going to say before the words left his mouth.

14

He sobbed now. Freely. And the words came pouring out.

"Cuz I'm all he's got, okay?"

He wiped the tears angrily with the sleeve of his hoodie.

"At least I have some friends. Chase has no one. I don't know why the kids are picking on him at school. He doesn't deserve that."

"Jake."

She was close enough now to reach out and touch him.

"Jake."

She reached around the sidewalk railing that separated her from the boy, gently placing her hand on his shoulder.

"Jake. Maybe you need to not do this—for Chase. Have you thought about that? I'm sure you have."

Jake started sobbing loudly and hugged the bar that he was hanging on to tighter.

"It's just so hard. Everything is so damn hard. I'm tired of it. I'm just sick and tired."

Laura knew exactly the tired that he was talking about.

"I know, Jake. I know. Can you climb over here by me now? Please, Jake. Let's just talk from here. I don't think you really want to do this."

"I dunno. So much shit has happened this week. I'm just sick of it."

He screamed the last words, and there were a lot more tears.

"What else happened? Can you tell me?"

"My girlfriend…well, I thought she was my girlfriend—totally dumped me for this other kid I know. What a bitch."

Laura could see the anger flash across his eyes in the moonlight as he talked.

"I'm just sick of everyone screwing me over."

His voice caught again and his mood seemed to shift from anger to sadness.

"The truth is...I really loved her. I didn't tell her but I felt like it was different with her, ya know. We actually talked about my stuff, which felt good with her. Now it just all sucks and I don't wanna see either of them."

"That does really suck. I'm sorry that happened."

She let the silence fill the air for a moment before she continued, willing him to believe her.

"Jake, I know this is hard for you to imagine right now, but it really is gonna get better."

The words echoed in Laura's head. *It really is gonna get better.*

"I promise. Nothing you are feeling right now is worth ending your life over. I know it's hard to see that but it's just the truth."

She tried to see his eyes from where she stood nearby, just on the opposite side of the rail now.

"Jake, will you look at me, please?"

He looked up at her, with tears streaming down his face. He had the dark hood pulled over his head but she could now make out the slight dark stubble on the face of a young boy who she'd guess had just starting shaving. And the dark eyes that looked up at her were kind and sad.

She swallowed back her own tears as the night's events struck her suddenly.

"How old are you?"

"Sixteen."

*Sixteen. God. Annie. He's only one year older than Annie.* Another prayer.

"Jake, you have your whole life ahead of you. I promise you it's gonna get better."

He looked at her and for the first time she sensed hope amidst the despair.

"Why do you think that? You don't even know me."

"Because I can see that you care. You don't want to leave Chase. I can tell that from the way you spoke of him. I'm guessing that you know that your mom and dad would be inconsolable too."

"Yeah, even though I feel like they hate me sometimes, I know it's not true. I just don't care most of the time."

*Annie. She cares too much.*

"Come on, let me help you climb over this railing."

She reached out with a tighter grip on his shoulder now and he didn't fight it.

He looked across the bay and took one deep breath before he turned his body and hoisted his leg over the railing.

Within seconds he was on the other side, standing beside her.

She moved forward with open arms and he let her hold him to her, sobbing as she hugged him.

"I never cry like this. God." He seemed embarrassed but he didn't fight the embrace. He needed the hug of someone who cared about him, and right now Laura knew that she was that person.

"Hey, no one needs to know, and I don't care about your tears. I do care that you are now on this side of the railing, and I do care that you are a fighter and that you have more courage than you thought you had."

Even as she spoke the words to Jake, her thoughts went to Annie and the necklace hanging in the car.

"Come on, let me give you a ride home and we can talk a little more in the car. Deal?"

He looked at her with a half smile.

"Yeah. I don't know why you ended up here tonight but I do feel better. It's kinda strange, actually. Okay, deal."

He reached out to shake her hand.

"Come on. Let's go." Laura tugged gently at his sleeve.

They began the walk back to the car in silence and it didn't seem to be uncomfortable. Just the way it was supposed to be. Laura was lost in her thoughts and she suspected Jake was as well.

She couldn't believe the way this night had turned out. For all of the last thirty minutes or so, she hadn't thought about herself or her own problems at all. It was interesting really.

Maybe she had just been taking herself way too seriously.

Well, not that she didn't have pretty big problems. She did. Nothing had changed. She still missed her old life with Greg. She still missed her old job at the marketing company and had no idea what to do next. But something had changed.

Maybe she could also get better.

She thought about her last therapy session. Had she been holding back? Was there more to talk about regarding her mother and her past?

She glanced at Jake, who seemed lost in his own thoughts.

God. What would have happened if she hadn't showed up when she did? Would he really have jumped?

She thought about how he looked when she first spotted him. The thought screaming through her head at the time was that that kid was minutes from jumping. And she believed it.

She reached out and gently put her arm around his shoulders as they walked the last few minutes it took to get to her car. He didn't resist, and she suspected it had been awhile since he'd let any adult this close to him.

She didn't really know why this young kid had come into her life tonight, but deep inside there was a quiet knowledge that the full scope of tonight's events would hit her later.

They came up to the lone car in the parking lot and at the same time took one last look back at the bridge and the city lights beyond.

Silence. Just the right amount of silence for a night such as this.

Laura opened the unlocked passenger door and reached for her keys under the seat.

She then reached across the passenger seat to unlock the door for Jake. As he opened the door, she cleared the seat of the note that she had placed there earlier, crumpling it in her hand as she slipped it in her bag behind the seat.

She looked over at Jake and for the first time that night she saw, in the same moment, not only his rough exterior but the pain of a hurt child. She placed her hand on his shoulder.

"It's gonna be okay, Jake. It really is."

She started the car and reached for the necklace that hung on the review mirror.

*Not today.* She thought to herself as she put the necklace around her neck.

She glanced again at Jake as she pulled out of the parking lot.

*Not today.*

# Missing You

Carly tucked the thick pink blanket tighter around Ella in the stroller as she noticed the wind picking up a bit, as it often did from the center of the bridge. She pulled her red knit scarf tighter around her neck. It was the one that Nick had given her last Christmas. He said that he loved the color red against her dark hair. She smiled at the memory.

She still couldn't believe how fast everything had happened.

The wedding had been amazing. Everything she had dreamed of as a little girl. All of their friends from school had been there, and her two best friends had helped her to plan every detail.

Getting married outside on the small stretch of sand that had the bridge as backdrop had been the perfect setting and introduction to their life together.

Carly reached into her bag, pulling out her favorite wedding picture from that day. Nick was so handsome, and in this picture he was directing his every bit of focus towards her in her white fitted dress and carefully made-up face.

*You are my princess,* he had whispered in her ear that day.

She gazed at the beach now from where she stood on the bridge as the memory overtook her. The setting sun made it look so quiet and peaceful, just as it had been that day almost two years ago.

She smiled as she looked down at Ella. The beautiful daughter that they had made together. She had Nick's blue eyes and a shock of dark brown hair. She was the best of both of them. Carly was sure of that.

"You look like your daddy, Ella." She bent down to kiss her daughter, who seemed content looking up at her and the massive structure of the bridge overhead.

Nick had been so heart-broken to miss her birth, but the video connection that they had the day after was surprisingly good, and she saw the tears in his eyes when he saw his daughter for the first time.

Carly's heart ached with missing him as she remembered. She hated that he needed to be so far away from them but she understood his passion for wanting to serve their country. It was something she deeply admired about him. She would be a military wife and support his dreams and goals because she loved him.

And one year away was bearable. Well, of course it was difficult for both of them to accept that he would miss the first six months of Ella's life, but the pregnancy came fast and unexpected, and they would make do with the situation. They always had.

She smiled, remembering Nick's reaction when she had told him that they were pregnant. He had just gotten home from basic training, and she had the test wrapped up for him as a gift to open after dinner that first night.

*Carly, are you sure? Oh my God.* He grabbed her and hugged her close to him.

And they had had an amazing two weeks together before he left to go overseas. Discussing baby names, planning the nursery, making love.

Carly looked down at Ella, willing her to know the intense love of her parents. The intense love that her father had for her.

She flashed back to the earliest days of their relationship.

Nick's thick dark hair and bright blue eyes had stolen her heart from the moment she sat beside him during pep assembly so many years ago.

And it seemed they had been inseparable ever since that day.

It had started out as a friendship, but even then they both knew that their destiny was to be together. And she had so many memories of being with him on the bridge at this very spot.

All of her biggest moments with Nick seemed to occur here.

Back in those earliest years, shortly after they had become friends in junior high, she remembered a field trip that they'd been on. After enjoying the morning in Sausalito, there was time for a brisk walk across the bridge before heading back to school.

Carly and Nick were lagging behind the others, as was often the case, chatting away, typical for their easy friendship. As they walked along and the wind picked up a little, Nick suddenly stopped her, adjusted her knit cap just slightly and in the same moment took her face in his hands. It was then that Carly felt the first of many of Nick's sweet kisses upon her lips.

Everything changed after that single moment on the bridge that day. Carly was his. She knew it deep in her core. She loved this boy.

It was at that same spot a year later that Nick stood holding her hand, confessing his love with such sweetness, as only a young teen-age boy could do.

*I love you. God, Carly, I love you so much.*

Such sweet memories. Carly gazed at the cherub face of their daughter, now asleep in her stroller.

*Some day a boy will love you that much, Ella.*

Her thoughts went to a recent conversation she'd had with Nick across the miles. It was one of many after they had learned that their baby would be a girl. He was so funny and protective. She knew that it would be a small miracle if any young boy would ever be worthy enough to date his precious daughter.

Nick had chosen the name Ella after the grandmother that had raised him, and Carly loved the name. It perfectly suited the sweet-natured six-pound baby girl from the moment they had first placed her in Carly's arms. And she could hardly wait for Nick to hold his daughter.

The loud sound of sea gulls jolted her back to the present on the bridge. So many memories here, and she had already been thinking about the walks she and Nick would take together with Ella once he returned.

She flashed back to yet another memory of the two of them dressed up one evening with the city lights in the background and sounds of the bay beneath them. Dressed for the prom, they were quite the dashing couple. Nick in his tux, and she had picked out the loveliest red dress. He had told her that he loved the way she looked that night. It was here on the bridge, where they went to snap a quick photo with some friends, that he had leaned over and whispered in her ear.

*Some day I'm gonna marry you.*

She caught the gleam in his eye and nodded her agreement. She adored him so. She couldn't wait until they could really start making their plans for a future together.

And suddenly the future was now.

They graduated high school and started making their plans.

At the end of one day like so many others they had shared, they'd been taking a stroll across the bridge while admiring the sunset and talking about the summer, when Nick made it official.

Carly's dark shoulder-length hair tossed in the wind now just as it had that day when Nick proposed, down on one knee and timing it just perfectly with the setting of the sun and their favorite spot.

*Carly, my love. If you will say that you'll be my wife and let me love you forever, you'll make me the happiest man to ever walk this bridge or any bridge in the world. Please say you'll marry me?*

She held up her hand now, lovingly admiring the most perfect wedding ring set he could have ever chosen for her.

She'd had no doubts back then and she'd had no doubts since then, even as the miles stretched between them and hard times loomed ahead because it was so hard to be separated from him.

But she was with him forever, and no distance would separate their love.

Carly looked down at Ella, the tears flowing freely now as she reached into her bag.

"Your daddy loves you, Ella."

And as she lifted the small bag slightly to the wind, allowing his ashes to float to the bay he loved so much...

"I love you forever, my darling."

# Perfect Daughter

Janice pulled her phone out to text Becca that she would be on her way shortly.

*At bagel shop, picking up your usual. Will be on time. Love, Mom.*

She smiled after sending it because Becca was always laughing at her for signing her texts. She was still getting used to the whole texting thing, but she loved it because it was another way of being able to keep in touch with her daughter throughout the day. And this would be especially important when Becca left for college in the fall.

Janice's heart fluttered a bit, as it often did when she thought of Becca leaving for college. But she knew that everything had been leading to this, and she was so proud of her daughter.

"Janice, hi."

She looked up to see her friend Trish, and her face broke into a wide grin.

"Trish! It's so great running into you here. I've been meaning to call you."

"I know, same here. Can you believe how busy everything has become? Between running to Katie's softball games and helping John with his college applications for next year, I feel like I haven't had a moment to breathe. How's Rebecca doing? Is she excited about Stanford?"

"You know Becca. She has a million things going right now. She's finishing a great track season, and determined to get that number one spot in the division. And then there's graduation planning, and amidst all that she's juggling a lot of time with Adam."

"Ah, yes…the boyfriend." Trish smiled as if she could sense Janice's mixed feelings about it.

Janice and her husband Paul did really like Adam. He was a great student and seemed to be very driven. A good match for Rebecca on paper. But Janice couldn't stop her own fears from surfacing whenever she thought about their seemingly deepening relationship.

Janice knew what it was to give up on dreams. She had done that herself when she had gotten pregnant with Becca during her senior year of high school. Not that she had any regrets at all. She and Paul had created a very good life for themselves, and she would never trade her years as a mother.

But Becca was different. So determined and passionate about her dreams of becoming a doctor. And so much smarter than Janice had been at her age. And with Adam attending Berkeley in the fall, it did seem that it was a relationship that could make it through the college years if it was meant to be. Both the kids seemed great at juggling schedules, so she suspected that they could manage, even with school and Becca's track scholarship.

She paid for the toasted bagel she had ordered and turned to Trish before rushing out to the car.

"I'll call you later this week. Let's set up a coffee date soon, okay?"

"Great, yes. I'd love that. Nice seeing you, Janice."

Janice hurried to the parking lot and the black BMW that she loved so much. It has been a gift from Paul right after he had made partner four years ago. She smiled as she remembered his words and the look on his face as he surprised her that day.

*I know we've been through some tough times. You've been by my side through law school and more long working hours than any wife should have to put up with. You've been a better wife to me and mother to Becca than I ever could have dreamed of. Thank you for never giving up on me...on us.*

And it seemed his hard work had paid off.

There was a move from their modest apartment in San Francisco to a lovely little home in Marin County.

Becca was settled into one of the best private schools in the city, and she had excelled there beyond their wildest dreams for her. She had dedicated herself to track and had become one of the state's best long-distance runners. That dedication had earned her a full scholarship to Stanford in the fall.

On top of her grueling track schedule, she was also senior class president, and she seemed to spend every other waking moment with her boyfriend, Adam.

The two had become quite close this past year but they were both good kids. Janice and Paul didn't really feel the need to worry about it. Becca had always been so determined and dedicated to reaching her goals. It was something Janice deeply admired about her daughter.

Now, driving towards the bridge, Janice's thoughts were interrupted by the ding of the phone beside her, alerting her to an incoming text.

At the stoplight she glanced down at the quick text from her daughter.

*Great! Thx mom. C u in the parking lot soon! Love, Becca! LOL*

\*\*\*\*\*

Becca's phone dinged with a new text just as she was finishing her run on the bridge.

God, she loved to run here. It was one of her favorite places when the tourists weren't out in droves, making it nearly impossible to really get a good pace going.

But today was perfect. The car traffic was crowded for rush hour but the walkway was relatively quiet, and she had been able to keep a decent pace while running almost seven miles by the time she had gone back and forth a few times.

She did love the weekly date with her mom here. Sometimes Janice joined Becca for a run, and did surprisingly well at keeping up. Not tonight though. Becca had told her mom that she was anxious to get going, and her mom had agreed that she'd take a miss for a brisk walk after with Becca instead.

Becca took a deep breath as she stretched her muscles and looked out at the city skyline beyond the bay. She was trying to hold it together. She'd become very good at controlling her emotions and keeping her eyes focused on what lay ahead. She sighed.

She read the text from her mom, laughing out loud because her mom insisted on signing her messages. She was trying to get with the times, though, with her smartphone and all, and Becca did really appreciate that about her.

And the truth was, she really did love spending time with her mom. She felt a bit more mature than some of her friends, in that she did appreciate all of the things her mom did for her.

Her stomach grumbled as she thought about the warm bagel her mom would be delivering to her in just minutes. She was always concerned about how well Becca was eating, not that she had an eating disorder or anything like that. It was just that many days became so incredibly busy, and her mom knew her well enough to know that she wasn't taking the time to get in the calories that she needed for her intense training schedule.

Becca's mom had been her biggest cheerleader for as long as she could remember. And she didn't really feel pressured by her parents like some of her friends did. They were just always there, involved and supporting her. She suspected it was why she'd always felt so driven to achieve her goals.

Running had become a really big part of her life, and ever since she made the varsity track team during her sophomore year, she'd dedicated herself to the sport and being the best at it. And she really had a good shot this year. She'd taken more first-place spots than ever before, and so far her track scholarship to Stanford had been one of her biggest achievements. She smiled as she thought about it.

She did want to make her parents proud of her. To continue to feel proud of her. Becca's stomach knotted even as this thought came.

Her mom would be here soon. Becca took a deep breath as she continued to stretch and look out at the bay.

*****

As Janice pulled into the parking lot, she could see Becca stretching in one of her favorite spots at the end of the walkway.

God, she was beautiful. The setting sun caught her blonde wavy hair, and she looked like an angel as she stretched towards the sky. It was rare to catch her with her hair down around her shoulders like that and, as if on cue, she reached up to corral the locks into her more typical pony tail.

To Janice, Becca seemed delightfully unaware of her own beauty, and it was something that she adored about her daughter. She was as smart as she was beautiful and as driven as she was fun. Yes, they'd done well raising this child, she and Paul. Out of everything that had happened during their marriage and life together, Becca was by far the best example of their success and happiness.

Before she got out of the car, Janice noticed that Becca looked sad, which wasn't normal for the typically bubbly girl, and made a mental note to ask if everything was alright with her and Adam. They seemed to get along so well, but the few times that Becca had been upset this last year did have to do with their relationship, and Janice wanted to be sure that Becca felt she could come to her with any problems. She craved that closeness with her daughter, and always wanted to be the one that Becca would turn to if anything were wrong in her life.

Janice grabbed the warm bagel, got out of the car, and headed over to where Becca stood waiting.

"Hi, Mom. Whatcha got there?" Becca grinned as she eyed the bag in Janice's hand.

"First tell me what you had to eat today."

It was the normal line of questioning. Becca was ready.

"Well, this morning I had that delicious omelet that you made for me." She smiled mischievously, ticking off her fingers as she continued.

"Then there was the thermos of freshly squeezed orange juice that you put in my car to have while driving to school. I found the package of crackers and the apple that you had slipped into my backpack and had them before lunch. And I did manage to eat a slice of pizza in the school cafeteria before I remembered that I had vowed to go with the chicken salads this week. Oops." She grinned at her mother's expression.

"So, Mother dear, as you can tell I have not managed to starve for another day *and*, after the nice run I just had, this" —she took the bagel lovingly out of her mother's hand— "delicious bagel from *the* most wonderful mother is really gonna hit the spot! Thanks, Mom!"

She kissed her mother on the cheek. "I do appreciate you, ya know. Even though sometimes I am a complete smart-ass teenager." She saw the quick cringe from her mom.

"Sorry. Smart-aleck, I meant." She laughed.

Janice rolled her eyes. "You're lucky you're such a good kid. So, how was school today? Tell me about the physics test. Harder or easier than you thought it would be?"

"Mr. Thomas is getting easier on us in his old age." Becca laughed. "The whole test took me like forty minutes, and it was definitely not worth the four hours I spent studying for it last night."

"Well, you've got some great study habits in place for what it will be like in the fall. I don't think you'll regret knowing how to put the time in. I don't need to tell you that college is going to be a whole different ball game. I have no doubts that you're going to just keep doing as well as you are now." She reached over to give her daughter a quick squeeze.

Becca looked away and bit her lower lip as she hugged her mom back.

"So did you wanna go for a little walk…maybe to the center of the bridge? I can eat this while we walk. My calves have been bothering me a bit, so the walk will do me some good, I think."

"Sure. And next time include me in your run, okay? I really do want to get these last ten pounds off, and I run so much better when I do it with you. Lizzy is a good running partner, but half the time we seem to do much more chatting and stopping for breaks than get any amount of exercise done."

Becca laughed as she thought about their neighbor. "Aww, Mom, Lizzy has been doing so well with her weight loss. I think it's fantastic that you're encouraging her. But yes, maybe we'll even up our runs together to twice a week. That is, *if* you think you can handle it, Mother dear." She tilted her head and winked in that playful way that Janice loved.

"That's a challenge accepted, daughter dear."

They started together down the walkway.

It was still pretty quiet on the bridge. The tourists had mostly cleared out for the day and it was easy walking, unlike some days where one practically had to elbow their way to get to where they were going.

Becca was unusually quiet and seemed a bit pensive. Janice didn't know why, but it made her feel uneasy, like there was a secret between them; and Janice hated that feeling more than anything.

It was a balancing act, being a mother to a teenage daughter. And she knew that she sometimes walked a fine line between being an overbearing mom and being her daughter's best friend who wanted to know every detail of her life. For the most part, she thought that Becca did share everything with her. But she wasn't naive enough to believe that there couldn't be secrets too. She knew what it was like to be seventeen. She remembered those tricky months of her own life when her mom was the last person that she wanted to confide in.

"So, how are you feeling about the meet on Thursday?"

"Pretty good. I took first place against them a month ago and I'm feeling pretty strong right now."

"I'll be there for sure, and your dad says he's gonna try to make it too."

Becca smiled at the news. "Oh, yeah? That'd be great. We only have one more meet after that, and Dad hasn't made it to many."

"Well, I'm sure you have plenty of races ahead of you, and Dad and I plan to be your biggest fans next year at Stanford." Janice noticed that Becca seemed to cringe a bit at the mention of college.

"Mom, you know I really have no idea how it's gonna be next year. The competition could be way more tough, and who knows how much I'll actually be running."

Janice noticed something in Becca's face. She stopped walking and took her daughter's arm.

"Becca, you're gonna be amazing. Stanford wants you on their track team. You didn't beat out thousands of candidates for no reason. You do know that, right? What's up with this negative talk all of a sudden? It's not like you." Janice frowned as she looked Becca in the eye.

At her mom's words, the tears started coming. Becca rarely cried but she seemed unable to fight it now.

"Honey, what's wrong?" Janice pulled Becca over beside her near the rail.

*She really is under way too much pressure. Something needs to let up,* Janice thought.

Becca was sobbing now. It was so unlike her. Even as a small child, Rebecca had seemed so unusually put together and in control of her emotions.

*She gets that from you, ya know,* Paul had told her on more than one occasion. He was the softie of the three of them, which delighted the women in his life. They could always count on him to be the one needing a tissue during the movie because there was "something in his eye."

Now, as Janice hugged her daughter to her, a sudden fear gripped her heart. She looked out across the bay that she loved so much and felt every hope that she'd ever had for Becca, for herself, slip away. She willed it not so, but in her heart she knew it was too late.

Janice closed her eyes and remembered the fear in the young girl that she once was. All those years ago. She didn't have the mother that Becca had holding her now. She could be that safe place and comfort for her daughter.

"I'm sorry, Mom." Becca sobbed. "We didn't mean for it to happen." She looked at her mom now with the fear of the unknown in her eyes. "I'm preg—"

"It's okay, Becca." Janice interrupted and pulled her daughter close again. "Everything's gonna be okay."

Janice had to fight back her own tears now as she came to grips with this sudden new knowledge.

*I'd never trade my years as a mother.* She'd had this thought so many times over the years.

She hugged her daughter closer and felt Becca's lean body relax in her embrace. They were both crying now. Janice didn't bother to hold back her own tears. She knew there would be times ahead to be strong and hold it together, but that's not what Becca needed right now.

"Mom, I'm so sorry. I never wanted to disappoint you and Dad," Becca choked out in between her sobs.

Janice stepped away just a bit, creating a little space between them. Taking her daughter's hands in her own, she took a deep breath and willed her own tears to stop.

"Rebecca, look at me."

Becca lifted her face at her mother's instruction, not with the eyes of the self-assured young woman that she'd become, but with the scared eyes of a child.

"Your dad and I are so proud of you. You are, and have always been, the best part of our lives, and there's nothing that you could do that would change that." Janice's voice caught and the tears started once again.

"But Stanford, my scholarship—I've ruined all of that." Becca cried bitterly.

*Yes. It's true,* Janice thought, and she felt the disappointment like a punch to her gut. *God please help me to say the right thing.*

"Do you love Adam?"

"I do, Mom. I really do. I can see us together, but we're just so—"

And before the words had even left her lips, a new recognition dawned of this woman, her mother, standing before her.

"—so young." She finished her sentence and looked to her mom now for something else. For reassurance, perhaps.

"I know, baby. You *are* young. *And* you're smart, you're determined, you're loving. And ya know what?"

Becca looked at her mom now with the first sign of real hope in her eyes.

"You're gonna handle this the way you handle everything. And I'm gonna be right by your side." Janice pulled Becca to her for another embrace.

*Just like you always are,* Becca thought as a new level of appreciation for her mother stirred in her heart.

"Thank you. I really do love you, Mom. Just in case I don't say it enough."

Janice saw the complete sincerity on Becca's face, and with the look, a touch of her daughter's light-hearted youth already slipping away. She sighed and let the thought rest in its proper place.

"I know you do, honey. And I love you too. I'll always love you."

# The Secret

Nikki quickly wiped off the counter and took one last look around the modest kitchen. The smell of the freshly baked cinnamon rolls threatened to bring on a new wave of feeling homesick, but she didn't have a moment to dwell on it. The recipe was her mother's and as a child she had spent so many Sunday mornings in the kitchen of their sweet little country home baking with her.

She looked around her new apartment that she was still trying to get used to. There had been so many big changes over the past few months, and she was desperate to make this a home for herself and Matthew. She tried not to talk about how homesick she was feeling, because he was under so much pressure to do well at the law firm. Taking the new job and making such a big move across country had been a big risk, but she had vowed to support him when they got married no matter what.

She looked over at Riley, who was busy with his blocks in the living room.

"Honey, please help me pick up your cars. Mommy's friend Susan is coming over in a few minutes."

She continued to pick up the living room and fluff the few pillows that were on the sofa that they had found secondhand. Hardly used; she was proud of their find.

She picked up the toy cars, for the sake of saving time not bothering to harass three-year-old Riley again. He was such a sweet boy. She bent down to give him a quick kiss and allowed herself one moment to think about the second child that they had been trying to have for quite some time now.

She sighed when she thought about the visit they'd had with the fertility specialist last week. Being able to afford IVF was a huge selling point for Matthew's acceptance of the job. They'd be able to afford it now, and hopefully it would work right away.

The doorbell interrupted her thoughts, and she glanced in the hallway mirror to smooth her dark hair back into the low ponytail she had managed earlier that morning. She cringed when she realized that she hadn't changed out of the sweatshirt she'd been wearing while cleaning up the house. Susan was always so well put together, and it was still the early stages of their friendship. Nikki had instinctively felt that appearances were way more important here than back home. Another sigh, but no time to dwell.

"Susan, hi."

Susan stepped inside the door to give Nikki a quick kiss on each cheek. Nikki was still trying to get used to that, as it wasn't something they did back home in the Midwest.

"Nikki, it's so nice of you to have me over. I'm dying to see your place—" Susan said as she stepped inside the apartment.

Nikki tried not to cringe as she thought about the apartment tour that would take all of three minutes. She hadn't been to Susan and James's place in Marin yet, but another one of the wives from work had told her it was spectacular. Everything about Susan was quite spectacular, actually.

"Well, you know. It's a start…until we are adjusted here in the city—and so far I love the neighborhood. Thanks for coming all this way. I know it can be a trek over the bridge during the morning commute," Nikki said.

"Oh, no worries at all. I'm actually using James's driver today because he has a big meeting in L.A. And I have an appointment with my magic doctor here in the city at 10:30, so it works out perfectly." Susan grinned mischievously.

"Magic doctor? Should I ask?" Nikki laughed an easy laugh like one she would have had with her best friend Tammy back home.

Susan laughed also, and Nikki noticed her flawless skin. She really was so beautiful. Nikki didn't know her age exactly but guessed her to be about ten years older than herself. She'd probably be wise to take a couple notes.

"Ah yes, my magic doctor, the king of Botox. Darling, you don't think it's by chance that I keep my frown lines away? I've been going for ages, and honestly, you might consider it yourself."

Nikki tried to mask her shock that Susan would say something negative about her appearance. *God, where am I?*

"Oh no. I didn't mean that at all the way that I'm guessing, by the look on your face, it sounded. You have beautiful skin, and from what I can tell, not a wrinkle showing. My suggestion is purely about prevention. Darling, it's all about prevention, really." Susan winked as she made the last comment.

"Well, I'll have to see about that I guess," Nikki said.

*Good. She was not being the jerk I thought she was.*

"And how is it getting the kids off to school in the morning when you're coming into the city? Do they go to school in Marin?" Nikki really was very curious about Susan's lifestyle and how she seemed to juggle so much.

"Oh yes, getting Avery and Conner off and running is no problem, *because* we have our dear Julie." Susan laughed.

"Julie has been our nanny since the kids were small. God, I guess that is going on five years now, maybe. I completely trust her, and honestly, she sees the kids more than I do during the week—and I think everyone is okay with that. She's so good with them. Are you going to be looking for help with Riley? I can have Julie put the word out. She's got a lot of friends in the area and I'm sure she could help you find someone."

Nikki didn't hesitate with her response. "Oh no. I'm quite happy to be here with Riley. He's still so young and I know how fast the time will pass. At some point, I'm sure I will be needing to find some babysitters, though. So far, we've been using a neighbor girl during the few nights out we've had since we moved in."

"Well, trust me. Your schedule will probably start to fill up quickly. Just let me know, whenever you are ready," Susan said

"Will do. So, let me give you the quick tour and then I'll pour us a coffee."

Nikki led Susan upstairs for a quick peek in the two bedrooms and the third that they had turned into a small office.

"Right now Matthew is using this for his office space, but we really hope to be converting it to a nursery very soon." Nikki didn't stop to think before the words left her mouth.

*God, I really need to stop being such an open book with all of my business.* She flinched, waiting for Susan's comment.

"Oh, nice; so you are planning to have more children then? It was James that wanted our second. To be honest, I could have gone either way. I hated being pregnant and it was so hard to get my body back in shape afterward. I had my personal trainer working double shifts on me," Susan laughed.

*Don't tell her everything,* Nikki willed herself.

"Yes, well, we figure once we are settled and Matthew is feeling great at work, we'll start trying again. We both come from pretty big families and have really been wanting one ourselves."

"James says that your husband is a real asset at the firm. I'm sure he will do very well. And honestly, if James approves, that's saying a lot," Susan said.

Nikki thought she saw something flash across Susan's face as she spoke about her husband.

*Don't be nosy, Nikki.* She could hear Tammy's playful voice in her head and decided to heed the advice.

"Well then, should we have some coffee? I made my favorite cinnamon rolls. I just have to frost them. You're gonna die. They are *so* yummy."

"Oh, no frosting for me," Susan said as she eyed the rolls on the counter. "I'll just have one half of one plain, please. Honestly, sweets go straight to my hips. I usually only allow myself one indulgence on the weekend."

"Are you sure?" Nikki debated now about frosting her own roll, and somewhat reluctantly opted to also have one plain.

"Oh yes, I'm sure. Enjoy it while you can, girl," Susan said while giving Nikki the once-over. "You really do have a gorgeous body, but what's with the giant sweatshirt?" She laughed.

Nikki was a little taken aback that Susan seemed to be checking out her body, but she seemed genuine with her compliments.

"I know. I know. I totally meant to change before you got here. Speaking of gorgeous bodies—Are we still on for the workout at club this afternoon? I really do want to find a place to work out, and everyone at the office seems to love your gym," Nikki said.

"Oh yeah, I was gonna talk to you about that. When we were making plans, I had forgotten about the Botox appointment today. I tend to get a little red and puffy afterward, so I'd really rather not be seen by loads of people I know. Normally I don't leave my house the day of an appointment," Susan laughed.

She continued, "Would you mind if we instead met to go for a walk on the bridge? The weather is gorgeous today and I do enjoy the fresh air. I try to do that at least once a week, if you have any interest."

"Yeah, that will be perfect, actually. I have a friend in from out of town who's staying in Napa, so I'll be up there for an early lunch. Want to plan to meet around 4:00? Or is that bad timing with the kids' school pick-up?" Nikki said.

"Oh, not at all. Julie will pick the kids up after school. I'll plan to meet you in the parking lot. Would be great if you could maybe shoot me a text when you are leaving Napa. Do you want me to ask Julie if she would look after Riley for you today? I'm sure she wouldn't mind, and it would give you a chance to have some adult time with your friend. Not sure where you're having lunch, but in my opinion, it's not the best place for young kids," Susan said.

"Oh, I'm good, thanks. I do have the neighbor girl watching Riley here this afternoon." She looked at her good-natured son, still content playing by himself in the living room. "I hope he will be okay. I haven't left him for this long yet with anyone other than family back home."

"Oh, don't be silly. I'm sure he'll be fine. You know how kids are. Just have her put him in front of a video and I'm sure he'll forget all about you."

44

Nikki cringed a bit inside at her words. She knew that Susan was joking, but she also knew that their ideas of raising children were pretty much on opposite ends of the spectrum. She had no desire to be anything other than a full-time mom to Riley and hopefully at least one more child. The thought of someone else spending the majority of the day with him made her heart ache a little. She didn't know yet if having a nanny here was the norm or if it was just a part of what looked like a pretty lavish lifestyle for Susan and James.

She would stick to her decision about withholding judgment, though. She was only just getting to know them, and so far Susan had really been very good to her, showing her around and helping her with the in and outs of the office politics. There was a small group there and all of the guys were married, so the wives were at least somewhat friendly to one another.

She definitely didn't want Susan to feel judged by her. And she did like a lot of things about her. There were parts of her lifestyle that Nikki and Matthew had been dreaming of. The nice house, nice cars, and private school for the kids. And from everything she had seen so far, Susan and James seemed to have a good relationship. The four of them had been out do dinner on a few occasions and the banter was lighthearted and fun.

"Nikki, I hope you're not bothered by what I said. Sometimes I have way too big of a mouth. Which you'll get used to." Susan winked.

"Oh, sorry, didn't mean to space out there. Was totally thinking about something else," Nikki laughed.

"Anyways, thanks so much for coffee. I have to run. I'm gonna try to swing by Union Square before my appointment to pick up a few items Andre called me about," Susan said.

"Andre?" Nikki searched her memory for any prior mention of the name.

"Yes. Have I told you about Andre? I can set up a meeting for you, if you like. He's my personal shopper, and I've known him for years. He keeps an eye out for things as soon as they come into the shops and snaps them up for me." She laughed at her good fortune.

Nikki didn't know whether to be embarrassed at her lack of knowledge or just amazed that someone would pay someone else to snap things up at the shops for them. *Where am I right now?* She laughed to herself, thinking that she couldn't wait to talk to Tammy about these new tidbits of knowledge she was getting. *Will I ever fit in here? And, more importantly, do I even want to?*

"I'll be sure to keep that in mind when my budget quadruples."

*God. There I go again. Stop talking about your personal business. Susan does not want to hear about your budget issues.*

"Hey, between you and me, I'm sure that Matthew will be making as much as the rest of the guys at the firm in no time. And I'm talking more than enough for you to be able to hire Andre and get a little Botox once in awhile." Susan winked as she stepped outside the front door.

*I wonder how many rounds of in vitro we can get with that money?* Nikki willed herself to not think about that right now.

"We'll see about that when the time comes," Nikki laughed, giving Susan a small hug. "So I'll see you later this afternoon in the bridge parking lot. Good luck with the shopping and the Botox."

"No luck needed, darling. Just a high tolerance for pain, which I've mastered over the years."

Nikki thought she noticed a flash of something honest in Susan's eyes.

*Is she really happy?* she wondered as she waved and stepped back inside.

She brushed away the thoughts about how the morning coffee with Susan had gone as she went into the living room to check on Riley.

"Riley honey, remember Janie from next door?"

Riley thought for a minute and nodded. "She plays ball with me at the park."

"Yes, that's right. She's gonna come over again in a little while and play with you while Mommy goes to meet her friend. Do you wanna go to the park again? Maybe Janie can make a picnic lunch for you both."

Riley smiled in agreement, seemingly perfectly happy at the news.

*What a great kid. How did we get so lucky?* And with that thought came another on its heels…*He deserves a brother or sister to play with.*

Her mother would say that it wasn't luck at all, of course. She had raised Nikki and her brothers and sisters well. And so far, Nikki and Matthew were totally on the same page with their ideas about discipline and showing lots of love to each other and to Riley. The last thing either of them wanted, was to raise a spoiled child or one that did not respect them or other adults. She did worry about the influence that some of these wealthier families might have on them and their kids. It just might be more of a struggle than she had imagined.

She didn't take time to dwell on the thought. She was anxious to get Janie and Riley settled so that she could get on the road to Napa. She hadn't been there yet since the move, so she'd be counting on the GPS to get her to the right place. The drive was supposed to be beautiful, and she was looking forward to getting out of the city for a few hours.

She quickly changed into her lunch clothes and fixed her face with a touch of make-up. Halfway down the stairs she remembered that she would not be able to walk the bridge in her heels, so she turned back to grab her workout clothes and shoes.

*I don't wanna give Susan any reason to be annoyed with me,* she couldn't help thinking, and just as quickly the thought came—*Why do you care so much what Susan thinks? Just be yourself.*

The doorbell rang and Nikki rushed to grab her bag and purse, and then let Janie in.

"Hi, Janie. Thanks so much for coming today to watch Riley. He really likes you, and he's looking forward to playing at the park if you don't mind taking him."

"Hi, Mrs. Thomas," she said with a lovely youthful grin.

"Oh please, call me Nikki. It's fine. So I thought maybe you could make a picnic lunch for both of you to take to the park. You'll find plenty of lunch meat and food in the fridge. Take whatever you like for yourself. Riley's favorite right now is peanut butter and he can have some of the Goldfish crackers that are in the pantry. Please also have him choose a fruit. I left some money, all the phone numbers, and the keys on the counter. You can take him for an ice cream down the street later if you like."

"That all sounds great, Mrs.—I mean Nikki. I'm sure he'll be just fine, and don't worry about anything," Janie said.

"I'm sure too," Nikki said genuinely. She wasn't an overly protective mother, and had a very good instinct about Janie. "After lunch in Napa, I'm going to meet a friend around 4:00, so I'd think that I should be home by 6:30 or 7:00 at the latest. Do call me if you have any questions or for anything at all."

"Will do. Have fun," Janie called out after her.

Nikki stepped outside into the gorgeous day. She tilted her face up toward the sun thinking how nice it was to have something other than the more typical chilly days they'd had since she arrived in the city.

She struggled to remember where she had last parked the car. The hassle of street parking was one thing that she was having a bit of a hard time getting used to. Back home they'd had a garage, and parking in town was never a problem. Here there were parking permits to deal with, remembering her street-cleaning days, and being lucky enough to find a spot that wasn't five blocks away from their apartment. She'd already gotten a ticket because she hadn't realized that she had to move her car to the opposite side of the street one day a week. She added "pay ticket" to her mental to-do list.

Yesterday had been a good day for parking, and she'd found a spot for their older Land Rover right on their own street. She sighed as she tossed her workout bag in the back seat. They really did need a new car. This one was on its last legs and she knew it. She thought about Susan's Lexus, wondering if they would ever be able to afford something so nice. The fact that James had his own driver was a whole other level of wealth as far as Nikki was concerned.

As she started the car and drove away toward the bridge she willed herself to stop comparing everything she had with what other people had, especially Susan and James. The last thing that she wanted was for Susan to feel that Nikki was jealous of her.

*That's no way to start a friendship and you know it.* And she did know better. There were a lot of things that were way more important to her than silly cars, houses and money.

She smiled as she thought about Matthew while she drove across the bridge toward Marin. There had been an instant attraction when he had come into the salon nearly six year ago. She was twenty-six when they met and had been thinking that she was never gonna meet a guy in her small town. Matthew had been visiting an old college buddy at the time, but it turned out that he lived only an hour away. By the end of the haircut and several jokes, they'd made a date for later that night and the rest, cliche as it sounded, was history.

They fell in love fast, but continued to date for a year and a half before Matthew finally proposed, and they were married six months later. Nikki smiled as she thought about the wedding she'd planned for months with her mom and best friend Tammy. It had been everything she'd dreamed of as a little girl. And she was very supportive of Matthew's career in law. She was still working as a hairdresser in another shop once they got married and she moved into his house one hour away. Even that move had been a little hard on her because she was so used to seeing her mom and Tammy nearly every day. But they managed.

They had had long talks about Matthew's career and his desire to move to a bigger city to practice law. They both wanted kids and they also both wanted Nikki to leave her job as a hairdresser behind once they had their first child. Nikki couldn't wait to be a mother. It was all she had ever really wanted.

Remembering the past reminded Nikki that she had wanted to call Tammy this morning during her drive. It was only 8:30 in the morning back home, but she knew that Tammy would probably be up and getting ready for work. She was still trying to get used to using her ear-piece driving here, but she'd had one stop with a warning already, so had vowed to get into the habit. Besides, the law did make perfect sense to her.

As she waited for Tammy to pick up, she noticed how gorgeous it was on this side of the bridge. She really did understand why Susan and James would love it over here and bother to commute so much to the city. It really was beautiful and like a whole different world once you crossed the bridge.

"Nikki!" Tammy's familiar voice burst into her ear.

Nikki laughed, happy that she had caught her. "Hey, girlfriend, how are things? How much do you miss me today?"

"Don't even tease me. You know how much I miss our early morning coffee and gossip sessions. What's goin' on, big city girl? Tell me everything new and exciting. Oh, and before you do, it looks like I am gonna take that week off before Thanksgiving, so I will be able to visit—if you guys are still up for me coming?" Tammy said.

"Yes! Of course we are. I wish it could be sooner. Things are okay. I'm feeling a little less homesick but I do still have my moments. Right now I'm driving to Napa, though, and it is *so* gorgeous out. Maybe we can work in some wine tasting when you come to visit," Nikki said.

"Ooh, girl. You know I like me some nice red wine. It's officially on our list. What are you doin' in Napa today—and I take it Matthew is working?" Tammy asked.

"Yes. He's been working a lot, actually." Nikki didn't try to hide the frustration that she was feeling. She could always tell Tammy anything, and lately she'd been venting a lot to her.

"Well…have you talked to him about it? Did you two know about the hours before the move or are you feeling blindsided by it?"

"Yes. To be fair, he did warn me that it would be long hours to begin with. It's just hard because everything is so new, and I haven't really met a lot of people yet; so I'm feeling just a bit lonely, I guess," Nikki said.

"What about that woman you were telling me about earlier? The one married to the guy that Matthew works with?" Tammy asked.

"Susan. Yeah, funny you should mention her. We just had coffee at my place earlier and I'm meeting her later this afternoon for a walk on the bridge."

"So, how is she? Someone you could see being a good girlfriend? It sounds like you've been spending some time together. Although from what you told me last week, she does seem quite different from the people you normally hang out with," Tammy laughed.

"What was it I told you, again? There have been a few instances, for sure. Oh yeah, you mean about meeting her for lunch at that fancy French restaurant last week? God, I don't care how much money I can afford to spend on lunch, you can't tell me that eating snails is any better than the yummy five-dollar burrito I found a few blocks from where I live. I really don't care if I ever have that again." Nikki giggled at the memory. "I seriously hope that she didn't notice me spitting them into my napkin as we ate."

Tammy laughed on the other end of the line too. "Well you can take me to your favorite Mexican spot when I'm there and I'll treat us to the margaritas."

Nikki winced as she thought about all of the fun nights they'd had out together back home. Margaritas, shopping, coffee dates and lots of good gossip sessions. Not that she gossiped in general. She would never tell other friends the things that she shared with Tammy. She didn't actually like people that did that at all. But they'd been best friends since high school and had vowed to always tell each other everything.

"I can't wait to take you out for a meal. Really. It could not come fast enough. I'm trying to make friends, though. I really am. I need to. I mean, we're committed to being here and I want Matthew to be successful at work. If that means sucking it up for a little bit while he has to put in long hours, so be it," Nikki said.

"And you and I both know that the increased salary is going to help a lot with your goals to have a family." Tammy knew Nikki's struggle and did not mince words. Nikki had shared with her that the decision to take the job and make such a big move was largely influenced by their current fertility issues and the desire to be able to try some more expensive treatments.

"Yep, you're right. I think I needed to be reminded of that today. It's funny because I look at Susan and James and everything that they have. They are probably the wealthiest people I know. Fancy cars, a big beautiful home in one of the more prestigious spots in Marin County and their two kids go to the best private school around. They sure seem to have an amazing life. Do you know that I found out just this morning that Susan regularly gets Botox, uses her husband's driver and has a personal shopper that pulls all the great new clothing for her as it hits the shops downtown? What land am I living in to be hanging out with someone like that?" Nikki laughed at the words coming out of her mouth.

"Yeah, but Nik…how do you know how happy they really are? I mean, someone who gets Botox on a regular basis does not strike me as a woman who is happy with herself. Ya know what I mean?" Tammy said.

"Yeah, I get what you're saying. It's weird, though. about Susan. Sometimes I feel that way too, but other times I have to remind myself to not be too quick to judge because I've had some real moments with her also. She has been a good friend to me, really. Going out of her way to show me around and make regular plans with me. And the few times I've been around her and James together, they seem pretty happy and normal. We do definitely have some different views on raising kids. God, with her nanny working so much, it sounds like she hardly sees them during the week. But for all I know, that's pretty normal around here. Tammy, if you ever hear me talking about getting a nanny for Ri, please come smack me upside the head."

"For sure, but that's not gonna happen. You're one of the best moms I know. A change of location and more money is not going to change that, Nik. It's just gonna help you have that family that you've always wanted. Speaking of which…how is my little Ri guy?" Tammy asked.

Nikki smiled at the nickname that Tammy had given Riley when he was just a baby and used ever since. The two of them were buddies, and he'd be very excited to learn that Aunt Tam was coming for a visit.

"Awww, he's great. Thanks for asking. He's such a happy little guy." She couldn't help but grin broadly as she said it, her heart swelling with love for her son. "He's spending the afternoon with the girl next door, who has babysat for us a couple times already. She's actually really great. I'm quite pleased to have found a sitter so quickly."

"That's great—and yes, Ri guy is a happy little buddy. I miss him a lot."

Nikki could hear a touch of sadness in her voice.

"And we miss you. A ton. I really can't wait for you to come visit, Tam. That really just made my day."

"I can't wait either. It will be a blast. And on that note…I gotta blast out of here to get to my 9:30 appointment. Mrs Ryan. You know how punctual she is," Tammy said.

"And grumpy when kept waiting." Nikki laughed. "Okay, go scoot. It was great talking to you, Tam. I miss you."

"I miss you too. Hugs to the munchkin. Bye."

"Bye."

Nikki clicked off the phone, feeling both happy and sad at the same time. It was great to talk to Tammy. She always felt better after their regular conversations. She could already hardly wait until she'd come to visit. They would have a great time, and she'd save some of her exploring to do for when Tammy was here.

Nikki's GPS did not steer her wrong as she found herself driving through the sweet town of Napa. It really was beautiful here. She thought again about all the long hours that Matthew had been working, and vowed to get him to commit to a weekend away with her. She knew that he would love it, and both of them did enjoy a good glass or two of wine.

She found the restaurant easily with just a few minutes to spare. Her friend Kate had chosen it and it looked very nice. As she walked up to the hostess, she noticed that Kate was already seated inside.

The hostess guided her through the plush interior of the restaurant.

"Nikki, it's so good to see you." Kate rose from her seat to give Nikki a hug.

They had known each other from beauty school, and Nikki hadn't seen her for several years.

"I was so happy when you called me last week to tell me about your vacation. It's great to see you too. Are you and Tom having a good time?" Nikki said.

"Yes, we love it here so much. It's beautiful, and of course you know how different it is from back home." Kate laughed as she nodded at the restaurant.

"Yes, I do know this and I'm still trying to get used to living in the city. It's different than over here though. I definitely need to explore this area more. It's so beautiful."

Nikki and Kate enjoyed a great meal of specialty sandwiches and sparkling wine, easily talking for a good two hours before Nikki looked at her watch. She wasn't sure how the traffic would be heading back towards the bridge this time of day, so she was trying to be mindful of her 4:00 plan with Susan.

"Well, I hate to end our chat but Tom and I have a couples massage scheduled for 3:00, so I better be heading back," Kate said with a big grin.

"Oh, no worries at all. I need to be heading back now also. Lunch is my treat, Kate. It was great to see you."

Nikki grimaced inside, not knowing where that offer had come from, because she was already stretching the budget just a bit this month. Perhaps she'd picked it up from lunching with Susan so much, who never let Nikki pay a bill.

"Are you sure, Nikki? That's so sweet of you."

"Absolutely." Nikki nodded as she got up to give Kate a big hug. "Enjoy the rest of your vacation. Tell Tom I said hello and let's keep in touch."

"Definitely. It was so good seeing you."

Kate left and Nikki paid the bill. On the way out to her car she remembered that she needed to change into her workout clothes. She was pretty sure that there wasn't a place to do that in the bridge parking lot, so her best option seemed to be the restrooms inside.

*Oh well. No one knows me here*, she thought as she looked at the crowded parking lot, thinking how out of place her workout clothes would look to everyone here at the restaurant.

She unlocked her car, and as she was reaching into the backseat she noticed a couple just a few cars away from where she was parked.

*Oh my God.*

With her heart beating wildly she quickly closed the door and ducked down a bit in the driver's seat so that she wouldn't easily be seen. She could hardly believe what she was seeing, and hoped like crazy she was mistaken. But even as the thought came, the couple turned just enough so that she could definitely make out their faces.

*Oh God. Please don't let them see me here.*

It was Susan's husband, James, and the woman he was talking to was Beth Ann, the pretty young secretary from the office. Nikki had met her and they'd spoken on the phone a few times when she had to call Matthew at work, but other than that, she didn't really know much about her.

*Maybe they are just having a work lunch,* Nikki thought and willed it to be true. But she knew that there had been a reason she felt so uncomfortable when she had first noticed them together in the parking lot. They seemed to be engrossed in conversation and their body language seemed way too intimate.

*You don't know for sure, Nikki,* she told herself firmly. And just as the thought entered her head, she looked again at the couple to see them kissing and embracing quickly before they got in the car.

*Okay. That definitely was what I thought it was.* Nikki felt sick to her stomach as she watched them drive off. *What am I gonna do?*

Glancing at the time, she quickly grabbed her bag and headed back in to change. She thought she might cancel her plan with Susan but just in case not, she'd better get into her workout clothes. She needed to think about everything she had seen.

*God. How do I get myself in these situations?* She felt almost angry as she changed, thinking about the dilemma she found herself in. They hadn't seen her. She was sure of that. So she could just keep it all to herself and no one would know.

*But would I want to know?* She couldn't even imagine Matthew ever doing that to her, and just the thought made her feel sick. She'd call Tammy from the car. She'd have some good advice for her, and then she could decide if she'd tell Susan at their meeting this afternoon, if she'd wait to tell her or wouldn't tell her at all.

She quickly finished changing and left the restaurant once again.

She climbed into her car and called Tammy as she was back on the road heading towards the bridge.

"Please pick up. Please pick up," she said out loud, willing her friend to answer.

"Wow. Two phone calls in one day, Nik. Great," Tammy buzzed in her ear. "Are you calling to give me all the gossip about your lunch with Kate?" She laughed.

"Oh my God, Tammy. I'm so glad you answered. You won't believe what I just saw." Nikki was totally distressed now, thinking about the situation even more.

"What happened? Are you okay? Nikki, you're scaring me a little bit."

"Yeah, sorry. I'm okay. Everyone is okay. You know my friend Susan, right? The one we were just talking about earlier."

"Yes, the Miss I-eat-snails-and-get-Botox woman…"

"Right. Well, I just saw her husband with the secretary from work," Nikki said.

"Okay. And? By *saw* what exactly do you mean?" Tammy asked.

"I mean that I saw them together, kissing. Oh God. They were definitely together. This is so not good, Tammy. What am I supposed to do?" Nikki's voice rose a bit in distress.

"Wow, that is pretty intense. Are you thinking about telling Susan? Do you think she has any idea?" Tammy asked.

"I don't know. Should I tell her?" Nikki's heart pounded at the thought. "Just earlier today Susan told me that James was in L.A. for a meeting. God. I wonder if the two of them are just shacking up together here in Napa for the day. How awful, Tammy."

"Okay, take a deep breath. This is definitely a tricky situation. I can see why you're upset about it. Let's talk it through until you feel good about what you're gonna do. So you are meeting her in a little while, right?"

"Yes, we're supposed to be meeting for a walk on the bridge in about thirty minutes. Should I just call her to cancel? I could do that." Nikki started to feel a little calmer as she thought about this as an option.

"Well, yes, you could, but is that just delaying the inevitable?" Tammy countered.

"Oh God. I dunno. What would I even say to her?"

"Well, let me ask you this. If the situation were reversed—and we both know that Matthew would never do that, or he'd have my wrath to deal with—" Tammy laughed.

"Tammy, don't even say that. The thought makes me ill."

"I know. I know. But if it were reversed, would you want Susan to tell you? Would you expect her to?" Tammy asked.

"Well, it's not like we've known each other for that long or are great friends yet, really. That's the part that feels hard. I mean in our very hypothetical situation, if you knew something like that, I'd totally expect you to tell me. But you're my best friend, ya know." Nikki felt more hopeless about the situation as their conversation went on.

"So think about it, really. Would you want to know?" Tammy asked again.

"Yes, I think I would. I mean it's more of a respect thing, right? I know and like Susan enough that, even just as a woman, I wouldn't want her to be disrespected like that. By my not telling, it just feels like I'm adding to that insult. Does that make sense?" Nikki waited for Tammy to agree with her.

"Yes, it does. But just know that you could totally be putting yourself in the messenger-about-to-be-killed position. I mean I'm sure the news is gonna shock her and she might even feel embarrassed that you know this information. From the way you describe her, it seems like appearances are pretty important so it's hard to know how this might affect your friendship. I guess you need to ask yourself if that matters to you," Tammy said.

Nikki let Tammy's word sink in as she thought about the question.

"I guess I just need to decide what is the right thing to do. It seems like I should tell her, and I think I will. And then just let the consequences of that fall where they may in terms of our friendship. I mean, hopefully she will see that I'm only trying to be a good friend in telling her, right?" Nikki asked.

"Yes, I think so. Trust your gut on it. And it sounds like you have."

"Yes, I'm gonna tell her in like twenty minutes when we meet." Nikki's stomach dropped at the thought. "Oh I wish I just never would have seen them."

"I know. The situation sucks. Sorry, Nik," Tammy said with real concern in her voice.

"Oh well, you know me. I'll just get it over with and hope for the best," Nikki said with more courage than she actually felt.

"Alright then. Call me back later and let me know how it goes, okay?"

"Will do; say a little prayer for me, please. Seriously. This is not gonna be easy."

"Will do. Good luck. Bye, Nik."

"Bye, Tammy, thanks for being there."

Nikki suddenly realized that she had forgotten to text Susan when she was leaving Napa as she had promised. She took a deep breath and brought up the number on her phone.

*Just act normal. You're not telling her anything right now,* she thought as she waited for Susan to pick up on the other end.

"Nikki, hi. Are you running a little late?" Susan's cheerful voice buzzed in her ear.

"Hi, Susan. No, so sorry. I forgot to let you that I was leaving the restaurant. I'm actually only about twenty minutes or so from the bridge right now. But don't rush. I'm fine to just wait for you there." Nikki held her breath, almost hoping that Susan would cancel altogether.

"Oh, it's not a problem at all. I just need to get my shoes on and I'll head out the door. We should be there at just about the same time. I am *so* needing this walk right now. I think the fresh air will be good for my freshly done face." Susan laughed at her Botox reference. "Oh, and I don't really need to rush at all. James and I were supposed to be having an early dinner in the city tonight, but as it turns out he's stuck in L.A. for another business meeting tomorrow morning and Julie's got the kids for dinner, so I am footloose and fancy-free. Hey, maybe we should go for a drink after our walk?" Susan asked.

Nikki was doing her best to keep her voice normal when she replied.

"Oh, that sounds really nice, but I do need to get back after this. I told Janie that I wouldn't be late, and I really want to be there to put Riley to bed tonight. Matthew hasn't been getting home much before 9:00 lately and I think it's nice if at least one of us tucks him in at night, ya know?"

"Honey, you are talking to the wrong person," Susan laughed. "When my kids were that age, I was in the society pages even more than I am now. But that's because James and I were really trying to make a name for ourselves here. Now everyone knows us and we can be a bit more choosy about our social engagements."

Nikki was silent on the other end of the phone, not really knowing how to respond.

"Oh, please don't think I'm being boastful. I don't mean to be. Really. I'm just so used to these petty conversations that I have with other women that are all about being seen at the latest and greatest events around town. But I know you aren't like that, Nikki. And actually I find it quite refreshing and I really like that about you more and more. So I'm sorry if I'm sounding like a jerk. I don't mean to." Susan's voice sounded genuine as she waited for Nikki's response.

"Oh, I'm not bothered at all, really. You're just fine. Just keep being yourself. I'm cool with that. And I'll do the same. So I'll see you in about fifteen minutes, then?" Nikki said.

"Yep. I'm just heading out the door now. See you soon." Susan clicked off the phone.

Nikki took off her ear-piece and felt exhausted all of the sudden. Susan really was a piece of work. Nikki smiled, actually, as she thought about her. She did like her and found her to be quite a puzzle if she was being honest. She really didn't know how Susan was going to react to what Nikki was about to tell her. Would she be shocked? Angry at Nikki for not minding her own business?

*Well, I would be devastated if someone delivered news like that to me about Matthew,* Nikki thought for about the tenth time since she had witnessed the indiscretion in the parking lot. *Thank God, Matthew would never do that to me.*

She tried not to think about it too much for the remainder of the drive, but it was difficult not to. As she pulled into the parking lot by the bridge, she felt her heart beating faster just at the thought of what was sure to be one of the toughest conversations that she'd ever had.

She'd only had about five minutes to think about it before she saw Susan's Lexus pulling into the parking lot. Susan parked next to her and practically bounced out of the car.

"I'm so needing some fresh air right now," Susan said to Nikki as she was locking up her car.

"Oh yeah? I guess I could use a little fresh air myself, actually." Nikki hoped that her voice sounded normal.

"How was your lunch in Napa? It's so beautiful there, don't you think?"

"Yeah, it is very pretty, and it was great to see my friend. I haven't spoken to her for a few years so we had plenty to catch up on."

"Have you walked the bridge yet since you've moved here?" Susan asked.

"No, but it's been on my list to do. Matthew and I brought Riley here last Sunday but it was pretty windy so we didn't make it much past the parking lot. It's so beautiful thought, isn't it?" Nikki looked out across the bay toward the city skyline as she spoke.

"Yes, it is, really. I should appreciate it more than I do, I'm sure. Maybe we should make a weekly walking date. I like to mix up my workout routines anyways, and it's always nice to spend a little of that time outside. Take advantage of the days with no rain, at least. Shall we head out?" Susan said.

"Sure." Nikki could already feel her heart racing as she thought about the best time to bring up the dreaded topic of conversation, and she couldn't quite muster up the courage until they'd walked for a few minutes together in silence.

"So, Susan…about my lunch in Napa today. There's something that I need to tell you." Nikki's heart was pounding fast now and she felt like she was about to pass out.

*God, this was not going to be easy at all.*

But there was no turning back now. She'd already begun, and Susan was nodding at her to continue.

"Go on. The suspense is killing me. Really, Nikki, you can be a bit dramatic at times." Susan laughed at her and motioned with her hands to continue with her story.

*She's really gonna be blindsided by this.* Nikki wondered if there was a way to back-track, questioning her decision now for about the tenth time since leaving Napa.

Nikki took a deep breath and stopped on the bridge, stepping over to the rail to let the few people that were out walking pass them by.

Susan stepped over to the rail next to her, and now Nikki was almost sure that she saw fear or something else flicker across her face. "Well, go on, Nikki. God, you're starting to make me nervous, and it's a little bit annoying, quite honestly."

With one more big breath Nikki blurted, "When I was leaving the restaurant, I saw James in the parking lot with Beth Ann from work." She looked at Susan now to see the color leaving her face.

"Well, I'm sure they were just having a business lunch—"

*But she knows that he lied about being in L.A.,* Nikki thought, then interrupted Susan in the middle of her sentence.

"Susan, I saw them kissing." Nikki felt really horrible as she said the words, thinking that she'd definitely made a big mistake in telling her.

She waited for her to say something as Susan looked out across the bay with a kind of vacant look on her face.

"Susan, I wasn't sure if I should tell you but I thought that if it were me—"

Susan interrupted Nikki as she turned towards her with a look that Nikki hadn't seen from her before.

"God, Nikki. Don't be stupid. Do you really think that I don't know about the affair?" Susan said.

Nikki felt shocked, not quite knowing how to respond to the unexpected question. "What do you mean, Susan?"

"The two of them have been carrying on for a few years now." She looked at Nikki coldly as she spoke.

"I'm annoyed with him for not being more discreet. That was our agreement when I found out about them. The last thing we need is for our friends and social circle to be gossiping about our business behind our backs."

Susan looked Nikki in the eye. "Do I need to worry about this or is this something you can keep to yourself?"

"I—I—I…of course I won't talk about it to other people, Susan. But how can you be okay with this?" Nikki was truly shocked and tried to prepare herself for what Susan might say to justify the odd admission.

"Well, honestly, Nikki. Don't be so naive." Susan looked over at her with the expression of a parent who'd just caught their child doing something stupid.

"Men cheat. That's what they do. Don't think that your Matthew will be any different a few years from now. Hell, I've even had my little one-night flings while on weekend holiday trips with my girlfriends. We don't talk about it, and in the end we're both getting what we want.

"Do you really think I would ever give up what we've built together? Don't kid yourself if you think you'll be any different," Susan said.

Nikki was really at a loss for words now and she felt like she had been punched in the gut.

*Where the hell was she living and who was this person that she thought was going to be a good friend?*

"Susan. No disrespect to you or how you choose to behave in your marriage, but that is not something that would ever happen to Matthew and me. And honestly, I don't really wanna stand here and listen to you even talk like that anymore." Nikki felt the tears stinging her eyes as she fought to hold them back.

"Look, let's just forget that any of this ever happened. I'm sorry that you saw what you did today and I'm sorry if my words offended you. It's just that I have a little more experience than you do with the way things work around here. I'm just trying to be a friend to you," Susan finished and looked at Nikki with what seemed like genuine concern.

"Okay, I think I just need some time to myself right now. This is all just a little too much for me." Nikki felt her body shaking as she began to walk away from Susan towards the parking lot and the safety of her car.

She didn't stop until she had reached her car, and once inside she glanced back at where she had left Susan on the bridge. Susan had pulled her dark sunglasses on and was still stopped in the same spot, staring out at the city. Nikki watched her for a moment. Suddenly she did a few stretches and took off in a jog in the other direction.

*Just like nothing had ever happened,* Nikki thought. And finally she let the tears come.

She was sobbing uncontrollably when her phone rang. Glancing down, she saw that it was Matthew and tried to get herself together before answering.

In defeat, she finally just answered the phone sobbing into it. "Matthew?"

"Honey, are you crying? What's wrong? Is it Ri? Matthew's voice rose in a panic.

"N-no. Sorry. Everyone is fine. It's just that I really need to talk to you." Suddenly she knew she couldn't stay here…in this place.

"Honey, I need to talk to you too. I'm driving home right now. Nik, I think we've made a terrible mistake in coming here." He sounded apprehensive about telling her this news.

"Really?" A strange sense of calm filled Nikki's body now.

"Yes, I'll explain more when I get home. But I put in my resignation today. I know I should have discussed it with you first but—" He sighed as if he'd had the kind of day that Nikki had had. "Something happened at work today. I found out something about James and it just—oh, I dunno. Honey, this isn't the right place for me. For us."

Nikki smiled and in an instant remembered all the things she loved about Matthew. "Oh, honey, really? You have no idea how much I love hearing those words today."

"Yes, really. We're going home, babe. Where we belong. I love you and I'll be home in fifteen minutes."

"I love you too. More than anything. I'll see you at home." Nikki clicked her phone off and started her car.

Just as she was pulling out of the parking lot, she saw Susan running up to her car, waving at her with a big grin on her face.

Nikki didn't bother to wave back as she drove away.

Sign up at the author website to be notified of new release special offers.

PaulaKayBooks.com